Dalmatian in a DIGGER

by
Rebecca Elliott

Capstone Young Readers
a capstone imprint

He's scooping up dirt.

He's dumping it over there.

BRMMM BRMMM WHEEE

What's THAT noise?

BRMMM BRMMM WHEEE

It really made me jump!

BRMMM BRMMM WHEEE

Oh my gosh! It's a . . .

Camel in a CRANE!

BRMMM BRMMM WHEEE

She's picking up the logs.

Then lifting them up high.

BRMMM BRMMM WHEEE

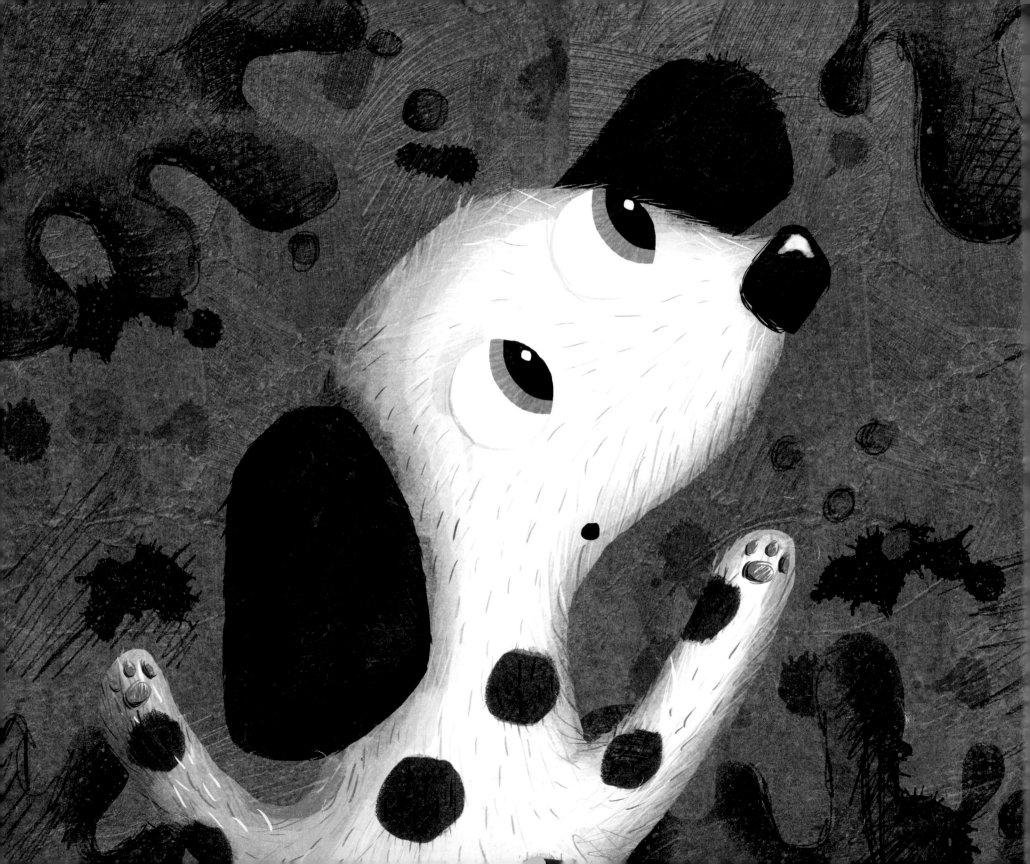

DUMP-SPLAT-CRASH

What's THAT noise?

DUMP-SPLAT-CRASH

It sounds really messy!

DUMP-SPLAT-CRASH

Oh my gosh! It's a . . .

TUG TUG BEEP

Now what's THAT noise?

TUG TUG BEEP

It sounds really BIG!

TUG TUG BEEP

Oh my gosh! It's a . . .

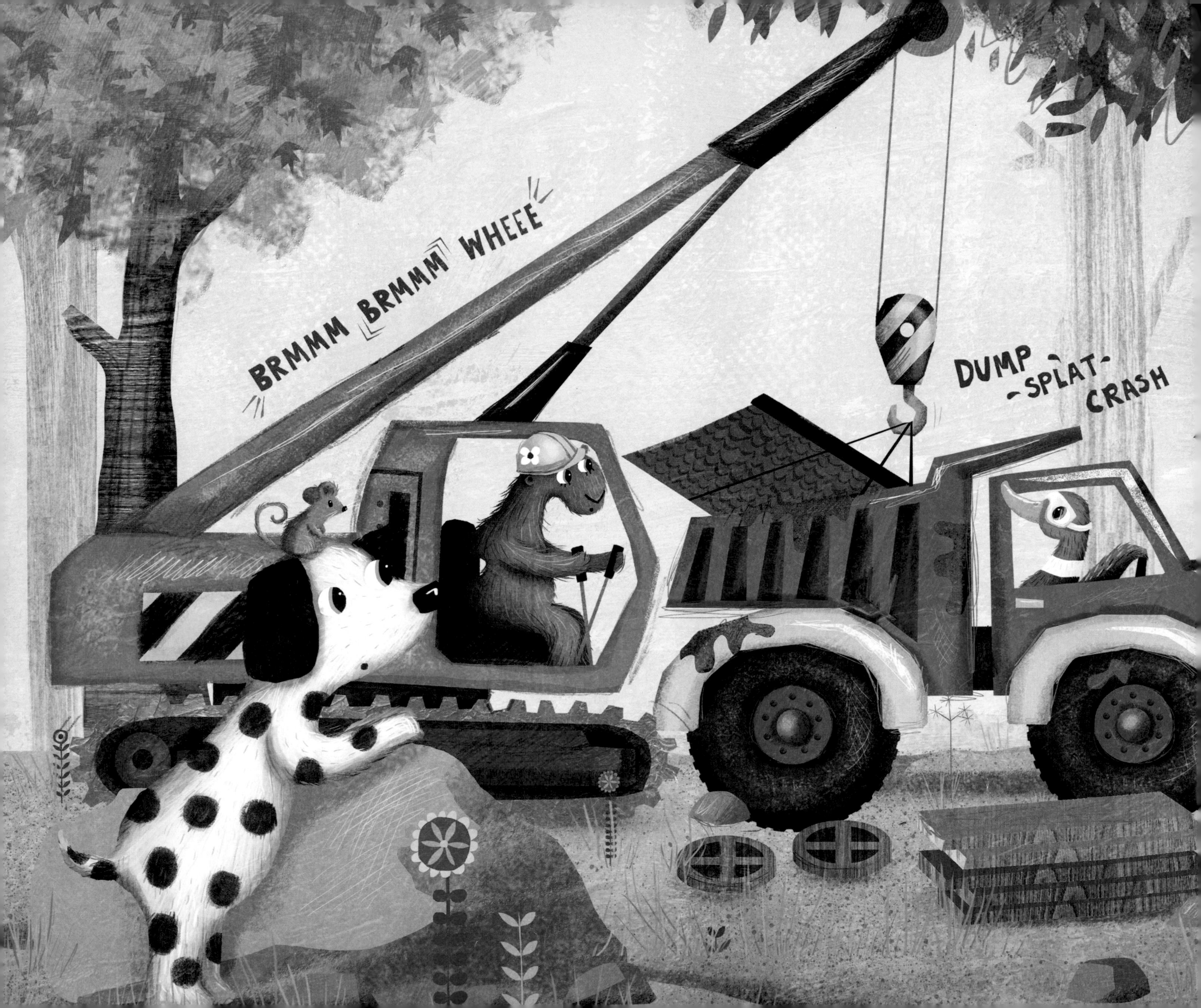
BRMMM BRMMM WHEEE
DUMP SPLAT CRASH

For Tom and Oli. May you never be too old for dogs and diggers. — R.E.

Dalmatian in a Digger is published by
Capstone Young Readers, a Capstone imprint
1710 Roe Crest Drive, North Mankato, Minnesota 56003
www.mycapstone.com

Library of Congress Cataloging-in-Publication data will be
availabe on the Library of Congress website.

ISBN: 978-1-62370-802-3 (paper over board)
ISBN: 978-1-5158-0684-4 (library binding)
ISBN: 978-1-5158-0685-1 (eBook PDF)

Designer: Lori Bye

Printed and bound in China.
009979S17

Hi! I'm Little Mouse.
I'm Dalmatian's best
friend. Can you spot me
throughout the book?